A RIPPING DAY FOR A PICNIC

A RIPPING DAY FOR A PICNIC

STORY AND PICTURES BY KEITH DU QUETTE

 VIKING

VIKING
Published by the Penguin Group
Viking Penguin, a division of Penguin Books USA Inc.,
375 Hudson Street, New York, New York 10014 U.S.A.
Penguin Books Ltd, 27 Wrights Lane, London W8 5TZ, England
Penguin Books Australia Ltd, Ringwood, Victoria, Australia
Penguin Books Canada Ltd, 2801 John Street, Markham, Ontario, Canada L3R 1B4
Penguin Books (N.Z.) Ltd, 182–190 Wairau Road, Auckland 10, New Zealand

Penguin Books Ltd, Registered Offices: Harmondsworth, Middlesex, England

First published in 1990 by Viking Penguin, a division of Penguin Books USA Inc.
1 3 5 7 9 10 8 6 4 2
Copyright © Keith Du Quette, 1990
All rights reserved

Library of Congress Cataloging in Publication Data
Du Quette, Keith.   A ripping day for a picnic/
by Keith Du Quette.   p.   cm.
Summary: Four fanciful creatures travel through caverns, a hedge
maze, and other magical places in search of the perfect picnic spot.
ISBN 0-670-08331-8   [1. Picnicking—Fiction.] I. Title.
PZ7.D9285Ri 1990   [E]—dc20   90-12164
Printed in Japan
Set in Caslon 540

Dedicated to

my hairy

friend,

Klaus.

It is a ripping day for a picnic.

Now proper plans must be made,

like who to invite?

Just give a hoot, a howl, a holler . . .

and wonderful friends will gladly greet you.

Next you must get the best things to eat.

So hunt and gather here and there . . .

and you will find delicious and tasty treats.

Now what a picnic this will be!

But there is one more thing,

that is, where to go?

Sometimes the right spot is hard to find.

Some places make you a bit scared,

while other places make you wonder,

how did this ever happen?

Who knows what you will find next

off in the distance.

So you set out for new places,

places which may seem just right,

but sometimes things aren't quite what they seem.

So the search must go on through thick and thin.

You never know what surprise awaits you,

or how wonderful it will be.

The world is a garden so full of delights.

With so much to see,

and so much to do,

that every day, is a ripping day for a picnic.

THE END